First Little Readers™ F

Tom's Lost Tooth

by Liza Charlesworth

ISBN: 978-1-338-29795-9

Illustrated by Tammie Lyon

First printing, June 2018.

 Published by Scholastic Inc. Printed in Jiaxing, China.

This is Tom.
Guess what?
He just lost a tooth.

Tom put the tooth
in a little box.

OOPS!
His cat knocked the tooth
on the floor.

OOPS!
His mom hit the tooth
with her broom.
It went out the door.

OOPS!
A man kicked the tooth
with his foot.

OOPS!
The tooth went into
a red wagon.

OOPS!
The red wagon hit a bump.

OOPS!
The tooth flew into a garden.

Tom looked and looked
for his tooth.
But all he saw was a squirrel
with a pile of nuts.

Guess what?
Tom finally saw his tooth.
It was in the nut pile!

OOPS!
The squirrel buried the tooth in the ground.

Tom dug and dug.
At last, he saw his tooth.
Hooray!

Tom grabbed the tooth.
He took it home.

Tom put the tooth
under his pillow.

OOPS!